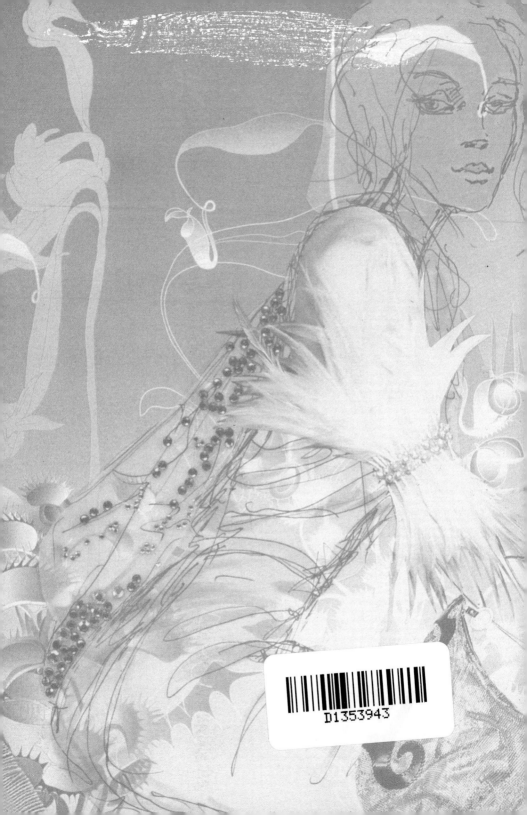

Since the dawn of time...

There have always been fairies; even before there were humans, there were fairies...

*Like the sea, the air and the wind in the trees, fairies **exist**. We've forgotten this now, but once, all humans believed in fairies and counted them as friends.*

8

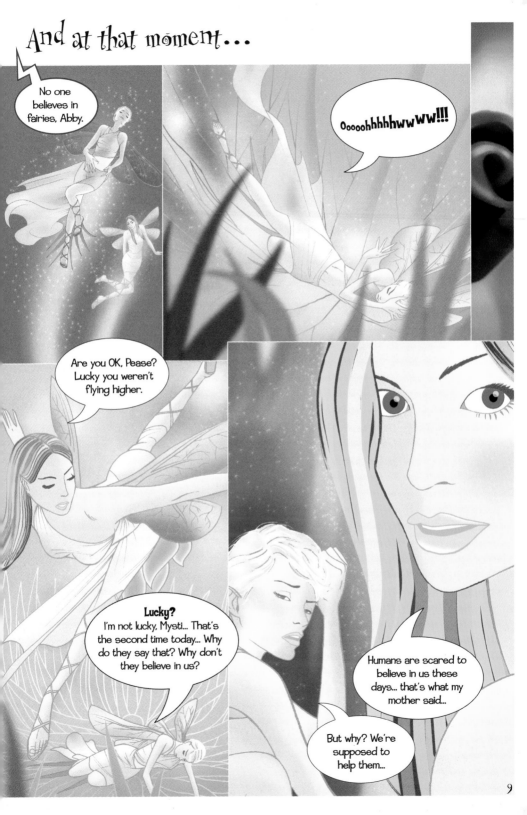

Hmmm. I don't understand either. But it's getting dangerous... you could have had more than bruises.

Mysti spots a fashion magazine lying on the ground...

I've got an idea. Stay here...

Dox garms for teenagers

Mysti, you can't! What if...

...and sprinkles  Gold Dust™ over herself...

Mysti! NO...!

i Gold Dust™

The most powerful magic fairy dust made from the dreams of baby children.

· If you sprinkle Gold Dust on a human - nothing happens...

10

Well... I might.

You should.

Oh yeah?

Yes. Because every time someone says they don't believe in fairies, a **FAIRY FALLS** from the sky.

 **Falling Fairies**

It's true! - And it all began in 1587 when Harold Skrimshaw, a miserable baker in Grimsby, threw a stale loaf out of the window and shouted, "There's no such thing as fairies!" in order to upset his wife. The loaf caught the unsuspecting Giselle Blueheath and brought her to the ground.

Look... do you
WANT ANYTHING?

i   Sarcasm

According to historians, sarcasm was
developed in the eighteenth century by
Gibbon (not a primate) in order for his
book *The Decline and Fall of the Roman
Empire* to avoid the censor. Although he
would have preferred to call it irony.
According to adults, sarcasm is the
lowest form of wit. According to
teenagers, it's a way of life, as important
as chocolate.

Want anything?

Yeah like do you
want to **buy anything**...
I mean this
is **a shop**...

Oh no... I mean... these
fairy costumes are so last
century and we never wear...
I mean **fairies** never
wear red...

(Dragons
wear red)

15

Are you sure?

That's all I need. Ella **BEING DIFFICULT** again.

YES. I mean, I should know... You're shredding my cabbage Mum! I'm not a flakking child.

Meanwhile on the Heath...

i Being difficult

Adults say teenagers are being difficult when they ask them a perfectly reasonable question and are given a stroppy sarcastic reply, usually followed by a swift exit.

Welcome to...

Until you've passed your Gold Dust Exam you are not qualified to be around humans...

i **Gold Dust Exam**

Very important GCSE (Gold Dust Certificate Special Exam) for fairies so they can become Gold Dust fairies and use the magic dust.

...We were just STRETCHING OUR WINGS.

Well I'll STRETCH YOUR WINGS if I catch you out there again...

i **Stretching wings and other threats from teachers**

Not strictly possible but all teachers like to finish your sentences in this way.

For example:
- I was eating a doughnut, sir.
- Well I'll doughnut you if I catch you at it again.

What if you'd met a **SHAPESHIFTER** or a **DROW**?

 Shapeshifters and Drows

Don't ask. Oh OK. More later. Maybe. It's not important at the moment. Can we just get on?

Welcome to Park Hill High...

...A grey stone building still trading on its illustrious reputation as a grammar school. The uniform is suitably dowdy and strict and the headmistress, **Miss Ogronski,** used to run a sweat shop in Borneo. In other words a natural for the job. You'll be glad to hear she doesn't feature in this episode. She is being questioned by the local police over a torturing incident.

Park Hill High School English Lesson...

ⓘ David Clopperfield and big prop magic

Hopefully none of you will know who he is. If you do, you'd probably hate him. You don't? Then you should! I mean, what's wrong with card tricks? This man made the Statue of Liberty disappear and flew 'without the use of wires'.

Like... yeah?

And while we're at it, if your boyfriend puts you in a box and tries to stick swords in you, he probably is David Clopperfield. Or wants to be. Either way chuck him immediately. Ask Claudia Sniffer.

ⓘ Evil Twins

Carly and Kaja think they are the coolest girls in the class and maintain this position by the sheer force of mega evil. Ella tries to ignore them but they manage to get under her skin all the same. Especially as they have big boobs. Both of them. No, both twins have big... yeah you get it. Even their boobs are identical. Apparently. They are tarty and popular with boys. You know why. All schools have evil twins. But they aren't always related....

25

Welcome to Fairy Hollow...

and Mysti's bedroom in Goldrush Hall...

You can take it off now.. and I want you to apologise to Professor Dust... I hear you were late today.

Mysti, we're not meant to be like them... we're different. Fairy clothes have evolved for a reason and we mustn't question it.

Later, on a fairy field trip...

Come along... Hurry up...

Now... I want you to observe the humans from a distance... Those of you with FAIRY GIRLS may watch over them. But take care. You are not to get too close, remember THE RISKS.

Humans: The risks

It is not easy being a fairy. You have to keep on your toes (and wings). Danger can occur at the most unexpected moment. For example:

Some humans carry lit torches...

They will rest without warning...

They are lousy shots...

Mysti... You will be graduating next week and the time has come for you to be allocated a human to watch over.

My own FAIRY GIRL?

Growing up means becoming responsible, Mysti. This is your chance to influence someone's life for the better...

Professor Dust looks into the enchanted pool to see the face of Mysti's fairy girl.

Who will it be, Professor Dust?

We shall see my dear... we shall soon see...

Ta da!...

You look great... is that for tonight?

Yeah... what about shoes though?...

You can borrow my kitten heel boots...

Really? Thanks... then I'm definitely getting this... What about you, El... you gonna get that?

It's not fair... I love it... but...

Don't worry... they'll grow... your mum has huge chumbas.

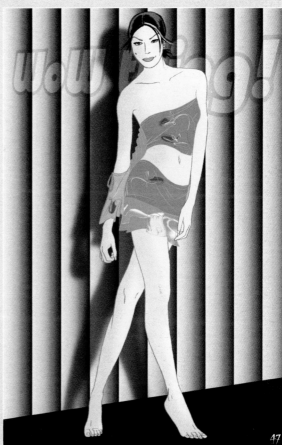

50

55

WOW...
Ella... that top's a bit tight... really does something for your figure...

Hey, you did go for the boob job then?

Ha Ha Ha... very funny. Go and die.

Oh... yeah... and this is Mysti... friend of Abby's...

55

Uh. Oh. Dad gets the car out...

Everyone else gets a cab, Dad...

And you get a chauffeur... aren't you lucky.

And Ella, you can have your mobile back for tonight... I know you girls can only communicate via text...!!!

I thought that was the one she...

He is...

Then why didn't she speak to him? Why was she...

Being cool? She can't let him know she likes him... that's the **RULES OF ATTRACTION**.

i Rules of Attraction

1. Find a really minging boy you couldn't fancy in a million years. Flirt with the minger in a really animated way in sight of the boy you do fancy (your target). The target will think you are really fun and exciting.

2. If your target tries to talk to you, act as though he is the minger and you wouldn't fancy him in a million years. Be strong. You can do it.

3. This way there is no risk if he thinks you're a gargoyle, because he didn't know you fancied him in the first place.

4. Be warned! Occasionally the minger will follow you home...

Oh-my-God... Will you look at Abby's friend dancing? This is RAP for flak's sake.

i Rap

Cool music.
Parents say there should be a C on the front.
How funny.

I don't mean to be rude, Mysti.. but everyone is staring at me... because of **YOU**. Can you dance with Abby? I just want to be cool.

That's not why they're staring. You wanted big chumbawumbas... well I've put a spell on them, just for tonight. **That's** why they're staring.

Really? So they can see...

Yes. **32 DD.**

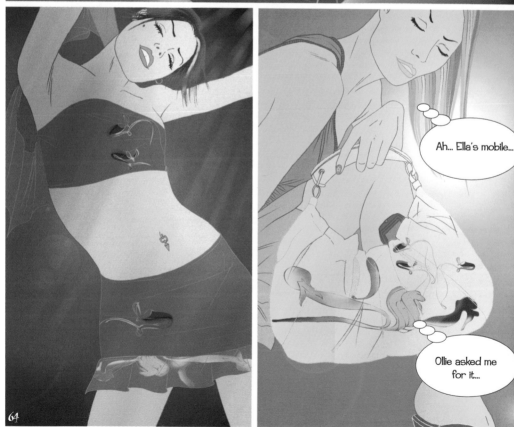

Noooooooō!!!!

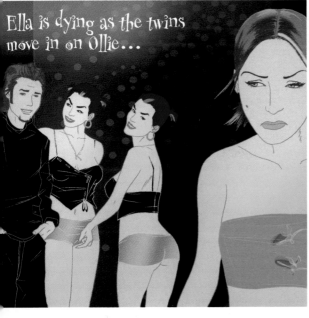

Ella is dying as the twins move in on Ollie...

Loads of partying later...

MYSTI RAINBOWFROST!!! What in the name of the Goldress was THAT?

Rap, sir. Great isn't it?

I'll "rap" you, young fairy. Now, fairy choir, again please...

Thy tooth is not so keen, Because thou art not seen, Although thy breath be rude...

73

Next morning...

Hi Abby...

Hi... where did you go?

Fairy choir... oh don't ask. I'd rather have stayed at the vent...

Well you didn't miss much. The evil twins smuggled in alcohol, threw up and tried to blame it on us. We had to go home early.

Poor Ella... she would have been disappointed.

Too right... And she lost her mobile.

I gave it to Ollie.

Why?

Oh Mysti, he her mobile... **number.**

He said he wanted Ella's mobile.

It's a movie...

Movie?

Yes....
magical pictures that
tell a story... with
music and...

But you have to
go as a human...
I'm sure that's
not the way...

I have to. Just this once.
Otherwise Ella can't go to
the magic pictures with
Ollie... It's not breaking the
rules, Pease... just sort of..
well, bending them really.

85

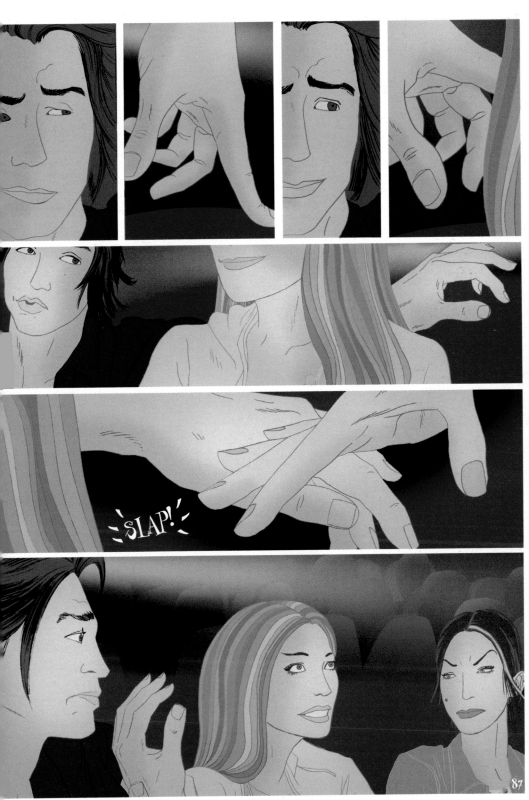

SLAP!

I know
Kung Fu...

12 Oxford Cross Whiteha
Westminster Camden
Golders Green

HAMPSTEAD HEATH

Quick, run...
There's
our bus!

Phew...
what the hell
happened
there...

WOW...
I'm gonna call
you Trinity...

To be continued...

Oh flak... you can't wait to
see what happens...?
OK OK turn over the page...